# Sunshine Home

*By* **EVE BUNTING** · *Illustrated by* **DIANE DE GROAT**

CLARION BOOKS / New York

*The illustrator would like to thank her models, Ellison Young as the grandmother and Emile Mosseri and his parents as the visitors. Much gratitude also to the director, staff, and patients at the Briarcrest Nursing Home, Ossining, New York, for their help.*

Clarion Books
a Houghton Mifflin Company imprint
215 Park Avenue South, New York, NY 10003

First Clarion paperback edition, 2005.

The illustrations were executed in watercolor on Bristol board.
The text was set in 15-point Goudy.



www.houghtonmifflinbooks.com

Printed in Singapore.

*Library of Congress Cataloging-in-Publication Data*

Bunting, Eve, 1928-
Sunshine Home / by Eve Bunting ; illustrated by Diane de Groat.
p. cm.
Summary: When he and his parents visit his grandmother in the nursing home where she is recovering from a broken hip, everyone pretends to be happy until Tim helps them express their true feelings.
ISBN 0-395-63309-5
[1. Grandmothers—Fiction. 2. Nursing homes—Fiction. 3. Old age—Fiction.]
I. de Groat, Diane, ill. II. Title
PZ7.B91527Sun 1994
[E]—dc20 93000570
CIP
AC

CL ISBN–13: 978-0-395-63309-0 CL ISBN–10: 0-395-63309-5
PA ISBN–13: 978-0-618-55157-6 PA ISBN–10: 0-618-55157-3

TWP 10 9 8 7 6 5

To Nannie
—E.B.

Mom and Dad and I are going to visit Gram. She's Mom's mom and she used to live with us. But she has been in the Sunshine Home for five weeks now and she'll be there longer. Maybe forever.

I haven't seen Gram since she fell and can't walk anymore . . . since the doctors said she needed full-time nursing care. I haven't seen her like that and I'm scared. I don't say so, though.

Dad and I pick sweet peas from our wire fence to bring to Gram.

Mom puts the new school picture of me in her purse to take with us. We're ready.

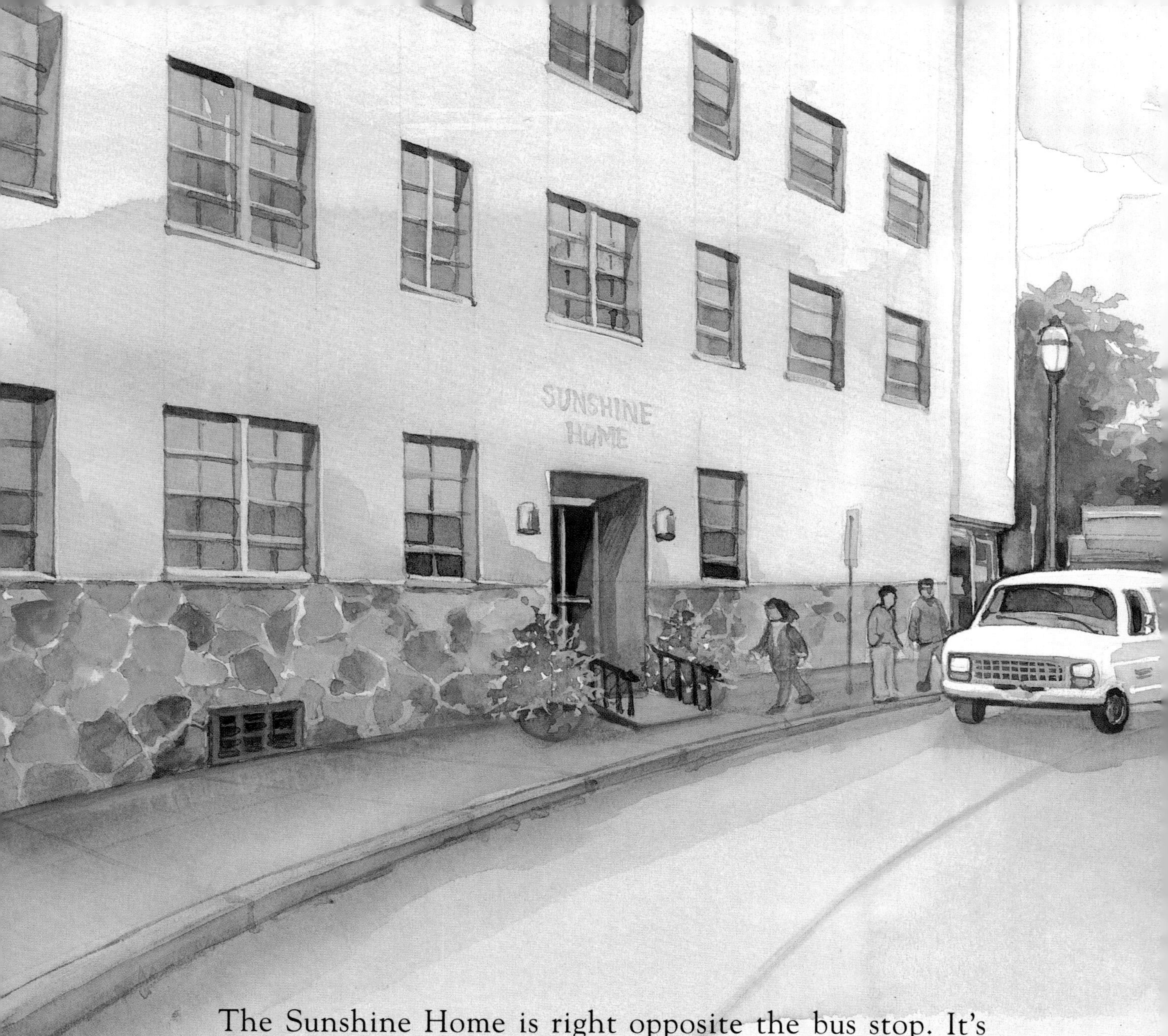


The Sunshine Home is right opposite the bus stop. It's square as a building block and it's painted barf green.

"Gross!" I say, and Mom says, "Stop that, Timmie. It's a very nice place."

There's a little market by the bus stop. Dad gets a bag of lemon drops for Gram and he buys a balloon that says LOVE for me to take.

It’s an embarrassing balloon and
I’m glad I don’t have to carry it far.

A ramp leads to the door of the Sunshine Home.

My stomach hurts and I want to run. Dad takes my hand. I pull back.

"What's wrong, Tim?"

"Well . . . ah . . ."

"Are you scared?" Dad asks.

I hang my head.

Dad squeezes my hand. "No need to be. Just keep remembering that this is Gram. She can't walk anymore. That's all that's different."

"Honest?" I ask. "She's still the same?"

"Honest," Dad says, and I feel better.

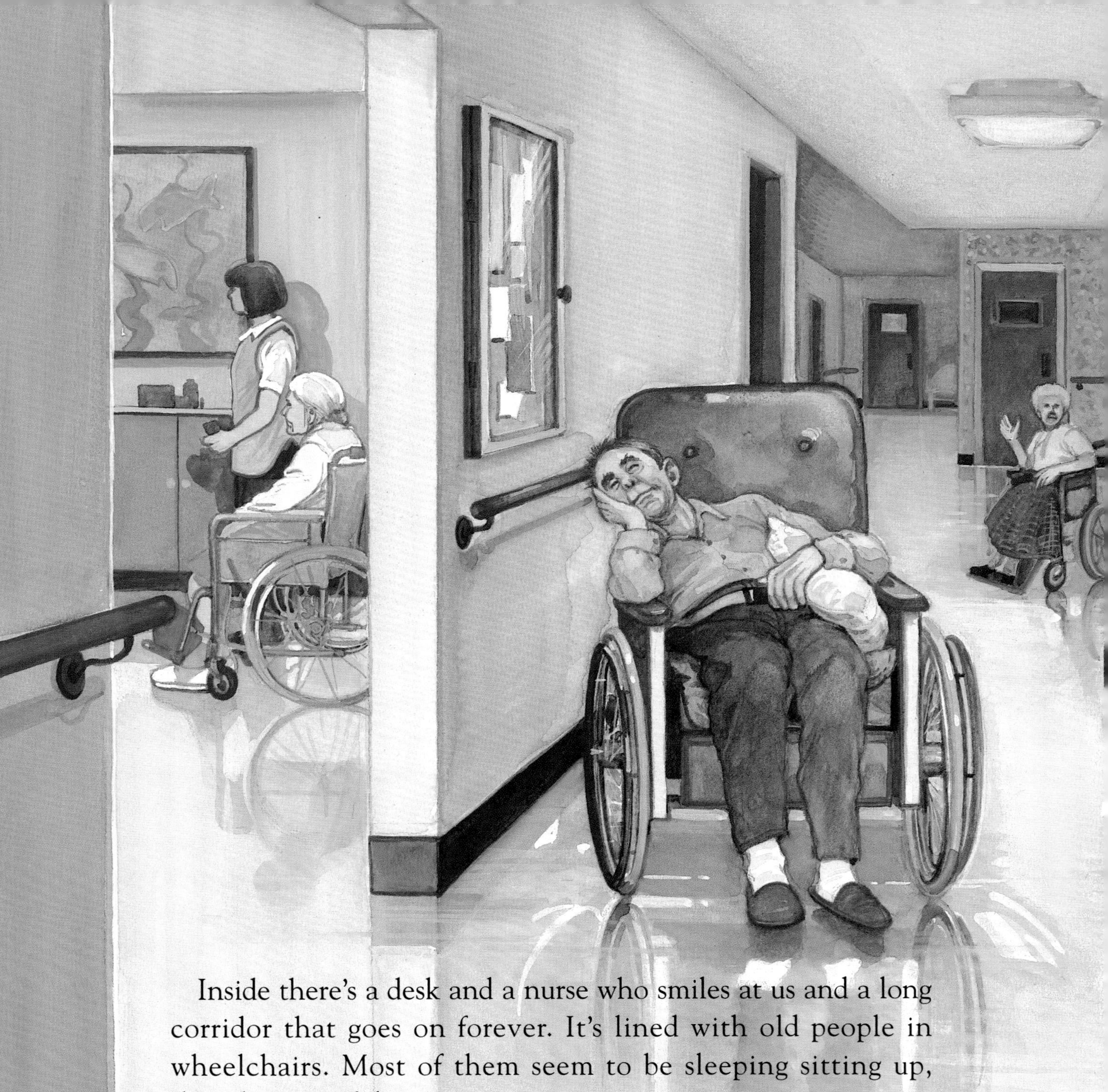

Inside there's a desk and a nurse who smiles at us and a long corridor that goes on forever. It's lined with old people in wheelchairs. Most of them seem to be sleeping sitting up, though some of them wave.

We wave back.

I smell an OK smell. It's like mouthwash, or the green bar that Mom hangs in the toilet bowl. The one that works for five hundred flushes.

"How nice and clean everything is!" Mom says to Dad in a voice I've never heard before, all bright and sparkly. I guess it's the one she uses in the Sunshine Home. "What *do* they do to keep this floor so shiny?"

It's shiny all right, like a mirror where the wheelchairs reflect themselves, upside down.

"There's Gram!" Mom's hurrying, with Dad behind her. I move more slowly.

Gram is in a wheelchair outside her room. She has a seat belt on. She's wearing a white sweater and her pearls and the blue earrings I bought her for Christmas. Dad was right. She's the same Gram except that her hair is curly instead of straight.

"You've had your hair fixed," Mom says, patting Gram's hand. "And your nails done."

Gram winks at me. "I'm some looker, aren't I? Hello, Timmie."

I kiss her cheek. She admires her gifts. Mom gets a vase from Gram's room and puts the sweet peas in it. She lets Gram smell them, then puts the vase back. Dad ties the balloon to Gram's chair. We all gaze up at it as it floats to the ceiling.

"LOVE," Gram says. "That's the best word there is. Thank you, Timmie."

Some of the other old people, the ones who aren't sleeping, have wheeled themselves close to share the company.

Mom and Dad say, "Hello, Pearl. Hello, Winnie. Hello, Charlie." They know everyone.

"This is my grandson, Timothy. He's seven," Gram says. "That Charlie Lutz is my destruction," she whispers to me. "He's a terrible driver. Always bumping me with his wheelchair. He shouldn't be allowed on the road."

I guess she means the corridor. I guess the road part is a joke.

Charlie Lutz is moving closer and I guard Gram's chair.

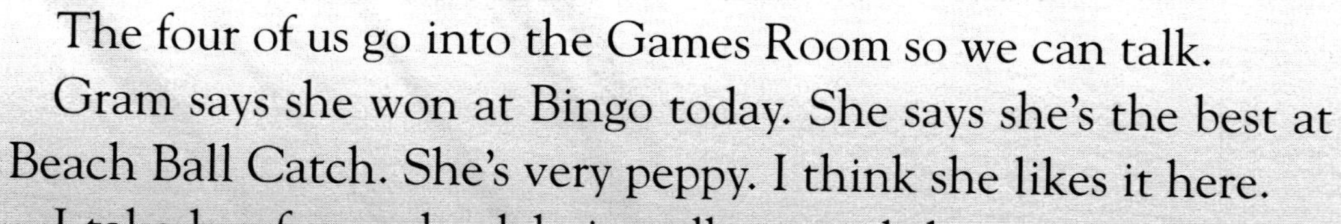

The four of us go into the Games Room so we can talk.

Gram says she won at Bingo today. She says she's the best at Beach Ball Catch. She's very peppy. I think she likes it here.

I take her for a wheelchair walk around the room and I stop at every window so she can see out.

She points. “There’s a finch, Tim.”
We watch it land on a branch, then skim away.
“Do the finches still come to the feeder outside my window?” Gram asks.
“Yup,” I say. “Ants come too.”

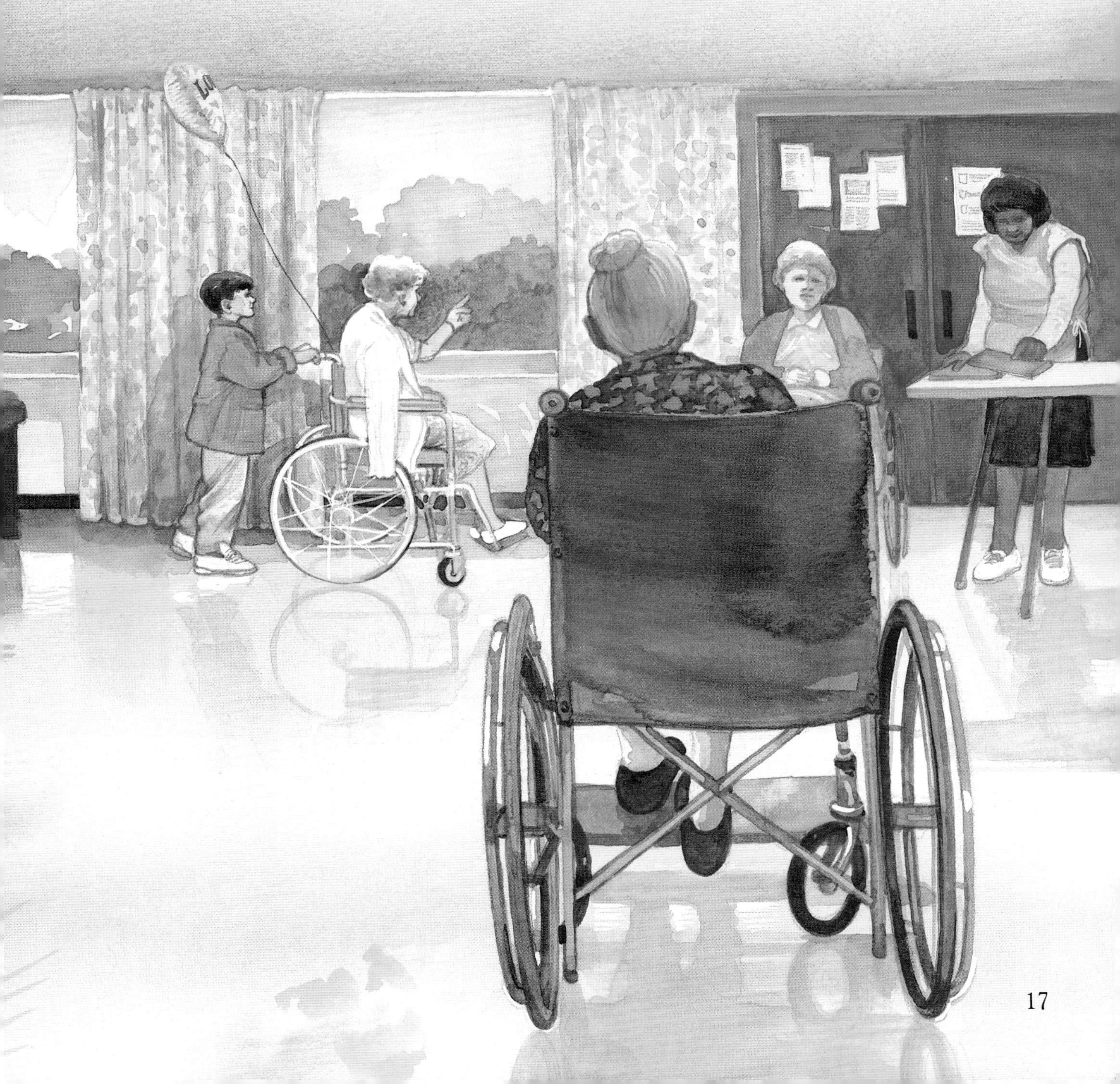

A nurse brings Gram's dinner and puts it on a table tray. He ties a big, blue bib around her neck.

I'm embarrassed for her. A bib!

I think Gram knows the way I feel. She gives me a nudge. "You ought to get one of these for your dad, Tim," she says. "It would sure save his ties."

"Your dinner looks good," Mom tells her, all cheery and chipper. I'll be glad when we're home and Mom gets her normal voice back.

"The food *is* good. Ice cream every day." Gram offers me the dish of vanilla but I shake my head.

When she's finished Dad unties her bib and rolls the table tray away. We get ready to leave. Mom fusses around. She asks Gram if she's sleeping well. If the new pillow she brought is all right.

"It's fine," Gram says. "Everything's fine," and her voice is cheery and chipper, too.

Going is hard. But there doesn't seem to be anything left to talk about. We don't want to leave Gram.

We kiss her goodbye.

"Come again, Timmie," she whispers to me.

"Sure." I'm choking up and I turn my head so she won't see.

Dad asks Gram if we should wheel her back out to the others but she says no, she'll just sit here for a few minutes. "That Pearl talks nonstop," she says.

We tell Pearl and Winnie and Charlie Lutz goodbye and they tell us to come back real soon.

The minute we're outside Mom bursts into tears and we have to stop while Dad holds her.

"Don't cry, Mom," I say. "The place is pretty nice. Clean and all. Gram seems happy."

Mom snuffles and lifts her head. "I even forgot to give her your picture."

I hold out my hand. "I'll take it back in."

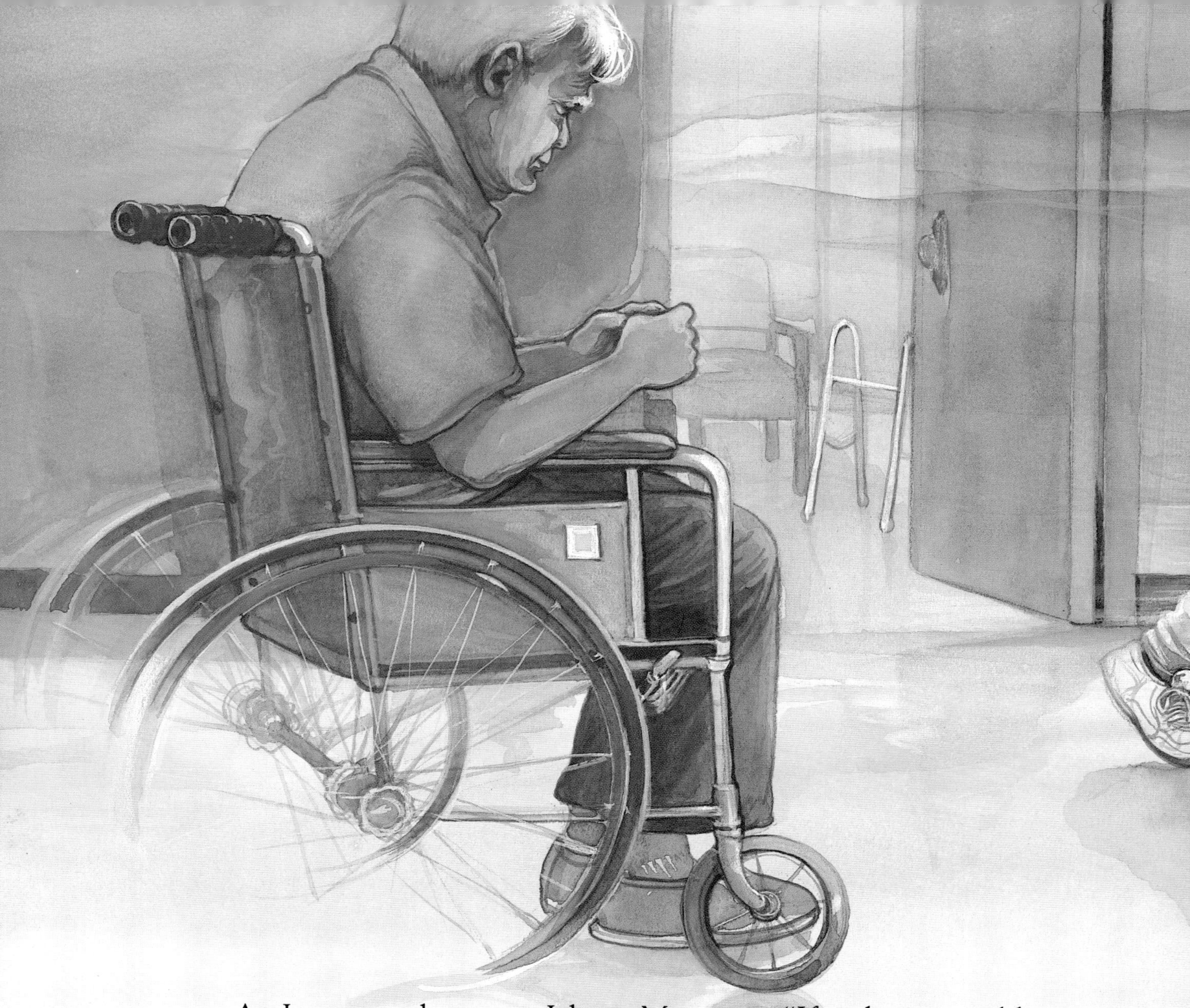

As I run up the ramp I hear Mom say, "If only we could bring her home. If only . . ."

I walk fast along the corridor.

Pearl chuckles. "You *did* come back real soon."

"Aren't you the boy who was here a minute ago?" Charlie Lutz asks, and I think he's kidding but then I see he's really puzzled.

"I forgot something," I mutter.

Gram's still in the Games Room. Her tray is where Dad left it, the bib on top. The balloon floats over her head and she's sunk so low in the chair that the seat belt is up around her chest. She's crying hard.

I'm terrified. "Gram?" I whisper.

When she sees me she tries to sit up straighter but she can't.

I go quickly and help her up. Then I hand her the picture. "Mom forgot to give you this."

She holds it at arm's length. "Nice," she says, and then, "I'm sorry, Tim. I didn't mean for you to see me like this."

I touch her arm. "It's OK."

"Don't tell," she says.

"You mean, don't tell Mom?" I'm beginning to understand things I didn't understand before. "Mom was crying, too," I say. "Outside. She cries a lot."

"She never does in front of me," Gram says.

"And you don't cry in front of her. You both pretend nothing's wrong."

Gram wipes her eyes with a little ball of Kleenex. "I guess we do it for each other, so it won't be harder than it is."

"No. No." Suddenly I'm sure. "It's better when you tell. Honest. You don't feel so scared." I edge backward. "Stay here!" Which is pretty dumb because where can she go?

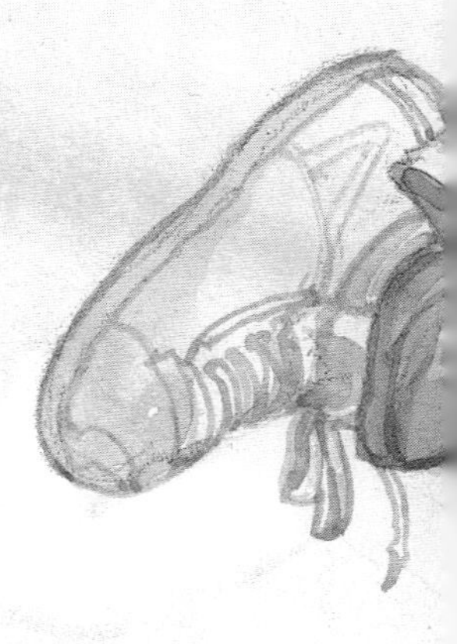

I race back outside. "Mom! Dad! Gram needs you."

"What? What's wrong?"

"Just come." I turn. Mom and Dad are running after me.

"Aren't you the boy . . . ?" Charlie Lutz begins but I don't take time to explain.

We stand inside the door of the Games Room and there is Gram, sitting very small and still. Tears roll down her face.

Mom rushes to hold her and Dad does too. We're bunched together saying things like, "We miss you so much."

And Gram's saying, "It's all right here. But oh, I wish, I wish I could go home."

"It's going to happen," Mom says fiercely. "We'll make it happen."

She strokes Gram's hair and Gram slumps against her for a minute. Then she pulls herself straight and says, "You know what, Tim? I'm really sick of this darn chair. I think I'll trade it in for a convertible. A red one."

"Look out, Charlie Lutz!" I say and we grin at each other and I feel better. But it's still sad. Because maybe Gram will never be well enough to ride in a red convertible. But maybe she will.

I look up at the balloon and I wonder why the word on it ever embarrassed me. It's the best word there is.